I0677590

ZEB GOULD
Destroyer Deliver
ALR024

Published by

Aqualamb

ZEB GOULD

Zeb Gould – Guitar, Banjo, Pedal Steel, Vocals
Jerome Begin – Piano, Keyboards, Vibraphone
Sam Crawford – Bass
Megan Gould – Violins
Jeff Hudgins – Saxophones, Clarinet, Vocals
Elizabeth de Lise – Vocals
Christian Rutledge – Drums

ALBUM CREDITS:

All String Arrangements by Megan Gould

Recorded at Dreamland Recording Studios, Hurley, NY
Produced by Sam Crawford and Zeb Gould
Engineered and Mixed by Sam Crawford

Assistant Engineered by Zachary Casper

Special Thank you to Nate Baker, Sam Crawford, Megan Gould,
Jerry Marotta, William Schaff, Friends and Family

All Songs ©Zeb Gould 2020

Cover art: William Schaff
Photo Illustrations: Aqualamb
Book design: Aida Aimer, Zeb Gould and Aqualamb

BOOK CREDITS
First Printing: Edition of 500
ISBN: 978-0-9985211-9-0

All Stories and Lyrics by Zeb Gould

Illustrations © by their respective authors and artists
All Rights Reserved

aqualamb.org
zebgould.com

Aqualamb

Destroyer Deliver

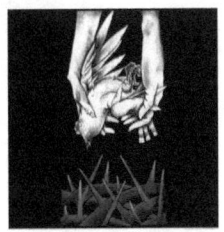

The music for *Destroyer Deliver*
can be downloaded via the link below:

aqualamb.org/024

PROLOGUE

"Ever since it happened, I've been dreaming," she said. "At first it was just a vague feeling upon waking, an urge. Every time I awoke, I felt something, but I could remember nothing, and as the days rolled away, my memory of the incident began to fade, but this vague feeling grew until it became an overwhelming desire. A desire I couldn't explain. A driving desire for us to risk everything and set out upon the sea. And as soon as we began these nighttime journeys, my dreams became vivid and I could remember everything." She opened her eyes, and began making circles in the water with her hands.

Tau sat up and looked at her small body floating in the massive sea.

Sela slowly righted herself, splashed a handful of water against her face, and swept the matted hair away from her eyes. She looked up at Tau, cast against the backdrop of the flashing barrier, then unspooled her body and rolled onto her stomach. With a few swift kicks, she propelled herself through the water, bringing her arms up over her head and down again into the sea with great power. He watched the trailing plumes as she circled the boat then clung to a rail at the stern. She rested here for a moment, and then let go and slid back into water.

The low sound of thunder rolled passed and the wind picked up out of the West as Sela laid back atop the waves, keeping her face above the water while submerging her ears; she wanted to feel her words, not hear them.

"I climb upward through a dense forest," she continued, "desperate to reach the top, because I know someone's waiting there. Over boulders and branches, through thick growth. I just keep climbing."

As a flash of lightning lit up the Western horizon, Tau caught a glimpse of the great bird as it passed above them, circling along its ceaseless path.

"I thought there was no end. I started to believe it was a never-ending slope, the same stones and the same branches in an endless loop." She paused and sat up in the water. "But I came to realize, the closer we get to the buoys, the closer I get to the top of the mountain."

Something about the way she spoke made Tau suddenly aware of the distance, of the isolation, of the fear. He felt the sickening effect of being bathed in red, bathed in black, bathed in red, bathed in black, endlessly. He tried to speak, but when he opened his mouth, he said nothing.

"Last night," Sela continued, "as I was nearing the peak, I stopped climbing, and sat down in the midst of a clearing to rest on the trunk of a fallen tree. For the first time, I took a moment to look at the mountain; to look at the rocks, the brush, the trees, the sky. And I suddenly realized that I knew this place; that I had always known this place. That I had been on this mountain forever. And I started to cry, not out of fear, but out of a deep sadness at the state in which the mountain had fallen. As my tears fell, all the colors of the mountain began to fade, and I felt as though I were about to awaken, but before the mountain could evaporate completely, I saw something: two yellow eyes peering out from behind a thorn bush. I called out to the eyes, and a large panther crept forth. It sat before me on its haunches, and spoke these words: 'You flood the folds and the valleys of my heart like an ocean.' I asked it everything, and it told me everything. When we were finished speaking, the panther lowered its body to the ground, rested its chin on its outstretched front paws, and fell asleep. But as I stepped around the great beast to finish my climb, I heard it crouch low behind me. 'Let me go.' I said, but the panther only crouched further, and in a harsh guttural tone, it said, 'All good things burn the best.' then it leapt towards me, and as it was about to strike, I awoke."

"What did the panther tell you?" he asked.

"Close your eyes and I will show you," she replied.

Despite all of his fears, the look in her eyes and the sound of her voice compelled him, so he laid back against the bow and closed his eyes.

When he sat up, he was alone in the midst of the clearing. Above him, the summit of the mountain was shrouded in mist. He looked at his hands and felt his face. Everything was unfamiliar, even the feel of his own skin, and he wanted the dream to end. The sky was turning a soft grey, and he felt from deep within that he must climb to escape, so he began to ascend, over stones, over branches, through the dense undergrowth of the mountain, until, at last, he emerged through a pine grove and found himself at the summit. There, laid out far below, he could see the town, and leading away from it, a long, narrow stone bridge that stretched out into eternity.

He looked to his right and saw the panther beside him. "Where is she?" Tau asked, and the beast turned to him, opened its great jaws and roared a terrible, deafening roar. Tau crouched and covered his ears as the sound boomed from the mountain and echoed off the great bridge. He looked below and watched the bridge shatter into jagged shards that fell away into a void, leaving the town suspended in nothingness.

When he turned back, the panther was stalking away from him and heading down the mountain, but as the first ray of morning streaked across the summit, the panther turned to Tau, licked at its enormous black paw, and growled, 'All good things drift away.'

With these words, Tau opened his eyes, squinting in the

DESTROYER DELIVER

sunlight that streamed from the East beneath a canopy of thick grey clouds, and fought to maintain his balance amidst the turbulent sea. Sela was gone, and from the West, the patrol was fast approaching. He yelled out for her, but a howling wind stifled his cries. As the small boat drifted into the long black shadow of a towering buoy, he looked up and saw her.

She clung to the great red dome as the surging seas rocked the massive buoy violently. She struggled to maintain her grip as the giant pendulum swung West, nearly touching the surface of the sea. In the moment before its rise, she readied herself, and as the buoy snapped upright toward the East, she let go, and propelled herself beyond the barrier. Beyond the great, red arc.

DESTROYER DELIVER

PANTHER ON THE MOUNTAIN

You start your fires like you're
lightnin' strikin' on the open plain
I hope they die by the morning and
spare all the beautiful things As
the lights of the city turn black
And the gates of the bridge
collapse you sing, "All good
things burn the best."

You flood the folds and the
valleys of my heart like an ocean
I try to find you by the stars but
I don't really know them
As the peaks roll away like the day
I hear the sound of your
voice in my head sayin' "All
good things drift away."

You were the panther on the
mountain that had me on the run so
long But you forgot about the lion
and the wolf and their beautiful song
As I leave you where
the sun is black
You lick your wounds, turn
your head and laugh, sayin' "All
good things come back."

PANTHER ON
THE MOUNTAIN

She really wants the toaster to speak first, because that would be the funniest way to start the story, but it doesn't seem to want to. She can hear the refrigerator's voice pretty clearly, but it's not very interesting, and the oven doesn't have much wit, so it really needs to be the toaster.

It has to be funny. Really funny.

Pencil drumming on paper.

Hmmm.

She drops her yellow pad next to the open cereal boxes on the table and heads for the transistor radio on the counter.

Static. Gospel. More static. Sermon. More static.

(W-I-B-C call sign theme music)

WIBC is on the air.

Ladies and Gentlemen, it's Sunday morning and you know what that means! It's time for, Exercise in Knowledge! (audience applause) Brought to you by the good people at Meadowbrook Insurance. (Sung) It's sunny today, but rain is on the way. Stay high and dry with Meadowbrook. And now, here's your host, Bob Greggson! (audience applause)

Welcome back Ladies and Gentleman. We hope you've had a pleasant and safe week. Today's matchup pits last week's winners, Cardinal Ritter, against our new challengers from Brebeuf Jesuit.

Let's have a big hand for all of our student contestants! (audience applause) Okay. Hands on your buzzers.

For ten points. The light we see from the sun comes from which layer of its atmosphere? (Buzzer)

Jerry, from Brebeuf.

The photosphere.

Correct! (Audience applause)

Did you know the sun had an atmosphere?

She glances quickly from the toaster to the fridge, then jots down the first words that come to mind, but she immediately scribbles them out.

For ten points: What Greek goddess was associated with an owl?

(Buzzer)

Jerry, from Brebeuf.

Athena?

Correct! (Audience applause)

Damn. She knew that one.

A small black shadow stalks in from the dining room. "You hungry, Speedy?"

She pours some cat kibble in the ceramic bowl by the door, but the cat doesn't eat, he just sniffs the food, creeps quietly along the wall, and squeezes behind the refrigerator. She hopes he isn't getting sick, because that old cat has been acting out of sorts all morning.

(Buzzer)

Jerry, from Brebeuf.

The Incan Civilization? Correct! (Audience applause)

She doodles. First little circles, then larger ones, then something that looks a little like Saturn, now planets, stars, the solar system. It gets more furious by the second, culminating with big angry solar flares stretching out into eternity.

She flings the notepad aside, gets up, and walks out of the room.

Let's stay in here though, you and I, in the kitchen. The morning light is nice in here. It's those east facing windows above the sink. The living room stays dark until the latter half of the day, but in here, the sun streams through those thin floral print curtains and covers everything in a soft rose. It feels like you're in a strange, beautiful still-life. Besides, I can still hear her. She's just around the corner, in the living room. She's at the desk by the piano. I can tell because I can hear the dial on the rotary phone spinning.

"Adelaide Stevens, do you know what time it is?" (Laughing)

"No!"

(Laughing)

"They're all at church, but they let me sleep in, god bless 'em. When are you going back? Tuesday?"

"No, I'm not back till Thursday. How's Lubbock?"

"Uh huh."

"Quiet mostly. I saw my little brother's rock n' roll band last night." "They sound great! They played 'Rave On'!"

I'm just going to interrupt our eavesdropping for a second to see if you've noticed something. Do you see that cat up there? Look on top of the fridge. Behind the dusty nativity scene. Do you see those eyes? He's perched up there, waiting, but don't tell her. Just keep an eye on him.

"Ya know Addy, this whole leave I've been having the most fantastic dreams."

"Uh huh."

(Laughing)

"You fink!"

"Okay. Yeah, I'll let ya go."

"Oh. Did I tell you what Cary did?" "Okay. Remind me. It's a real doozy."

"Okay, lazy bones."

(Laughing)

"Okay, I'll see ya soon. bye."

Here she comes, remember not to tell her about the cat.

She sits back down at the kitchen table and tries to write a little something from the sinks perspective to see if she can find its voice.

Is the sink considered an appliance?

With her eyes closed in thought, Speedy's moment has arrived. That little black cat rises slowly and wiggles his little black hips. It's ready to pounce right into that big ball of knotty hair gathered on top of her head.

But, just as she's about to make the kitchen sink speak, and just as the cat is set to take flight, they both hear a noise.

It's the spring on the back porch screen door creaking and stretching.

Before she even hears the footsteps on the linoleum, she knows it's her sister Sadie trying to sneak in, so she creeps up to the door, lowers her voice, and in her father's slow cadence asks, "Where have you been, young lady?"

"Damnit Belle! Don't do that!"

(Buzzer)

Jerry, from Brebeuf. The pericardium? Correct. (Audience applause)

"Are you really just gettin' home?"

"Don't tell Mom and Dad."

"How was it?"

"You shoulda come with us."

"Did Eli meet up with you? He said he was gonna meet you guys."

"No. He finked out."

"Did you know that the sun has multiple layers to its atmosphere?"

"No, and I don't care cause I'm goin' to bed."

"I didn't even know the sun had an atmosphere. Hey, Sadie, wait. Imagine you're a toaster and say something funny."

"Good night."

"That's not very funny."

You haven't forgotten about that cat, have you? During that little conversation, he was crouched down behind one of the cobweb strewn three-wise-men, watching. He knows better than to strike while there are two of them down there. He's just biding his time, waiting for another chance.

How long can a common swift fly without landing? (Buzzer)

Jerry, from Brebeuf.

Ten months.

Correct. (Tepid audience applause)

Ten months? That can't be right.

Okay, enough stalling.

She stares intensely at the toaster and tries to imagine it making a declaration to the rest of the appliances. It's easing the tension? Yes, that's it. She'll start the story in the middle of some great conflict that's just happened, they're all sitting there silently, and then, the toaster breaks the tension with a really funny line.

She bends her head over the pad, ready to scribble away like mad, and the cat sees his opening. His perfect moment. So his eyes widen and he rears back on his haunches. His hips come up in the air and he shakes them slowly from side to side, ready to spring.

But suddenly, he stops, lowers his body, and sits like the Great Sphynx. Some people say animals have a sixth sense.

Ring!

She pulls at her hair and tries to ignore the phone.

Ring!

She was just about to write the perfect line.

Ring!

The perfect way to set the story in motion.

Ring!

"Speedy, what are you doin' up there?"

Ring!

"Damn."

Don't go with her into the living room. Stay here. And cover your ears because the sound she's going to make is too painful, and I don't want you to hear it.

Just stay here and savor this rose colored sunlight for a little while longer.

DESTROYER DELIVER

A BODY AIN'T NOTHING

A body ain't nothing but
The fate of a broken man
A body ain't nothing but the
blues A heart's gonna get around
The ways that we keep it down
A heart's got nothing left to lose
A body ain't nothing but
The fate of a broken man
A body ain't nothing but the blues

Shadows like mine stretch
on As far as the crow can go
Shadows like mine stretch on
to you Your arms get more to
hold Cradling my shadow
Cause a body ain't nothing but the
blues Shadows like mine stretch on
As far as the crow can go
Shadows like mine stretch on to you

A body ain't nothing but
The fate of a broken man
A body ain't nothing but the
blues A heart's gonna get around
The ways that we keep it down
A heart's got nothing left to lose
A body ain't nothing but
The fate of a broken man
A body ain't nothing but the blues

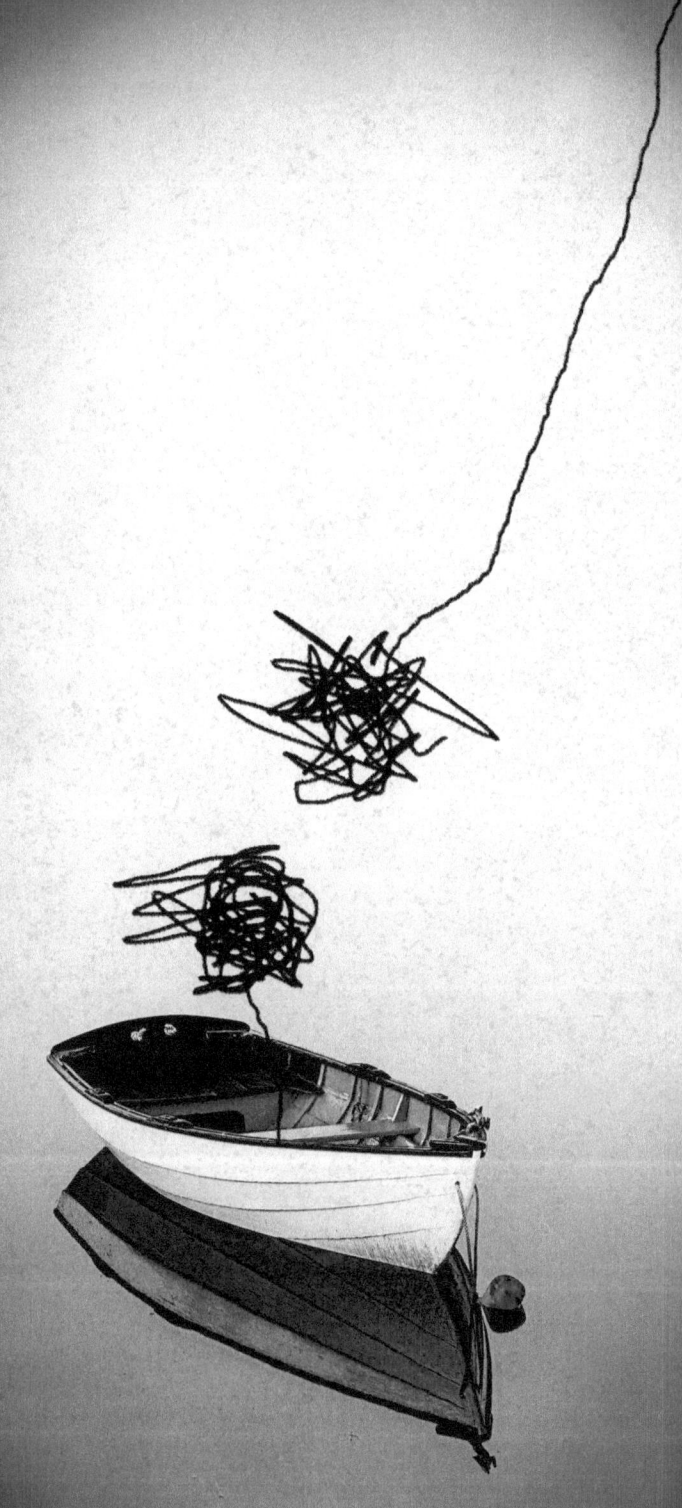

A BODY AIN'T NOTHING

The Cranford Fisher is the worst boat ever made. Those are fightin' words up there, but I'll say it again, the Cranford Fisher is the worst boat ever made, without question. I don't care if you print that. Have you ever ridden in one? It's got a flat bottom, shallow little sides, and a square hull. Don't wear nice clothes, 'cause if you drive into the wind, water's just gonna spill in and you're gonna get drenched. Worst of all, you hit a bad wake at a bad angle and you're liable to flip the damn thing over. They use to advertise it in all the magazines with a picture of some jerk perched on the bow, holding a chainsaw, while a few yards away, the stern is floating off. The whole idea being, you can cut the thing in half and it still won't sink. Who the hell needs that? I guess a Korean War vet, that's who, 'cause my Old Man bought one. Bought it hook, line, and sinker.

But, there is one good thing about the Cranford Fisher - It's light. That's why my sister and I took it, because we couldn't start a boat at the dock without waking up the whole camp, so we had to take something we could row a ways out into the bay before we could fire it up.

The electric starter didn't work. Even with the choke all

the way open, the thing wouldn't turn over, so you had to pull start it. Ever had to pull start a forty horse power motor? Might not sound like much, but it's hard. You gotta get some momentum going and pull with all your weight. I'd had a few, so I was having a hard enough time just standing up. The first time I pulled on the handle I nearly fell in the lake, but once I got my bearings I managed a few good pulls. Just as I was about to throw up, the thing finally turned over. It took me a minute to remember I had the choke wide open, so the thing roared like the dickens until I closed it up and let it settle into an idle. We didn't take off right away, I had to just sit there a minute.

Nighttime up there is scary and beautiful at the same time. Beautiful 'cause there's no lights, and when the stars are out you can really see 'em. You can even see the Milky Way, that's how dark it is. Scary 'cause once you push off the dock, it all looks the same. It's just a big circle of bent pine trees all around you, no channels, no inlets, just these wind blown pines all pointing you in the same direction. Even If the moon is shining, it's hard to know which way is which. That's why most people don't drive at night up there, even the locals.

And I'm not sure what kind of lakes you've been on, but the waters up there are treacherous. Tons of shoals just waiting to bend your prop to hell. In other words, you really gotta know your way around, you can't just get in and drive in a straight line from Point A to Point B unless you're sure there's not some huge rock sitting out there in the middle of that straight line. And usually there is.

There's one thing, and one thing only, that you can see at night up there - the Lighthouse. It's just a little red dot that hovers at the mouth of the Main Channel. It marks the entrance for the big boats that need to come in from the open water. And the nice thing about the Main Channel is, as long as you keep your bow pointed at the red light, you're in the clear as far as rocks go. If you really know your stuff, and you can keep yourself heading in a straight line, you can even blow right past the lighthouse and drive all the way out to the bell buoy.

Our place has a pretty clear view of the lighthouse, so once you clear the point of Blackberry Island, and the red light is directly ahead of you, you can go full bore.

We didn't say much, just looked up at the stars. On this night, it was cool, and the moon was about a quarter full, full enough to see a fair amount of stars and to see the reflection of the rocks off the smooth surface of the water. The mirrored image of those big rocks sloping down into the water look like big hands praying, and it always gives me the willies. Eventually, I chucked my empty over the side and slid the throttle into drive. As soon as the red light was in view, I gunned it.

It didn't sound like you'd think it would. Not like I'd think it would anyways. Not like in the movies. Fiberglass hitting rock makes a pretty dull sound; just an average kind of thud, even if you're going really fast. What I really remember is the sound the prop made when it came up out of the water. When those things have nothing to push against, they make an angry high-pitched whine. People say time slows down during an accident, so, all in all, I probably wasn't in the air for as long as I think, but it really did feel like forever.

Run your tongue up in front of your upper teeth. Stick it way up to where your gums meet your lip. You feel that? That tiny little ball of flesh that hangs there? I don't have one of those anymore. Must've smashed it to bits on the steering wheel. Aside from a few stitches, that was the worst of it for me.

Funny how you can be two things at once. I remember being scared as hell swimming around and yelling out for Gail, but at the same time, I remember feeling glad Belle stayed behind to keep an eye on the kids and put the baby to bed. It always took her a while to get the little one down because of his harelip. You had to jam that bottle way back in his mouth for him to get anything out of it. Took forever. He's stitched up now. He can talk and everything, but he's kinda hard to understand. It is what it is.

Honestly, I can't remember if it was cool. Most nights it gets cool up there, so when I'm telling this story, I always say it was cool, but truthfully, up until we got going, the only things I remember are Belle chucking her wedding ring at me as I stumbled out the door, and Gail shushing and laughing as she dropped her beer can onto the rocks right in front of The Old Man's cabin. The two of us freezing there, waiting for his light to turn on, that almost feels like it lasted as long as the accident. Feels like a lifetime.

Oh yeah, and I remember that Cranford Fisher just floating there, upside down. It never did sink.

DESTROYER DELIVER

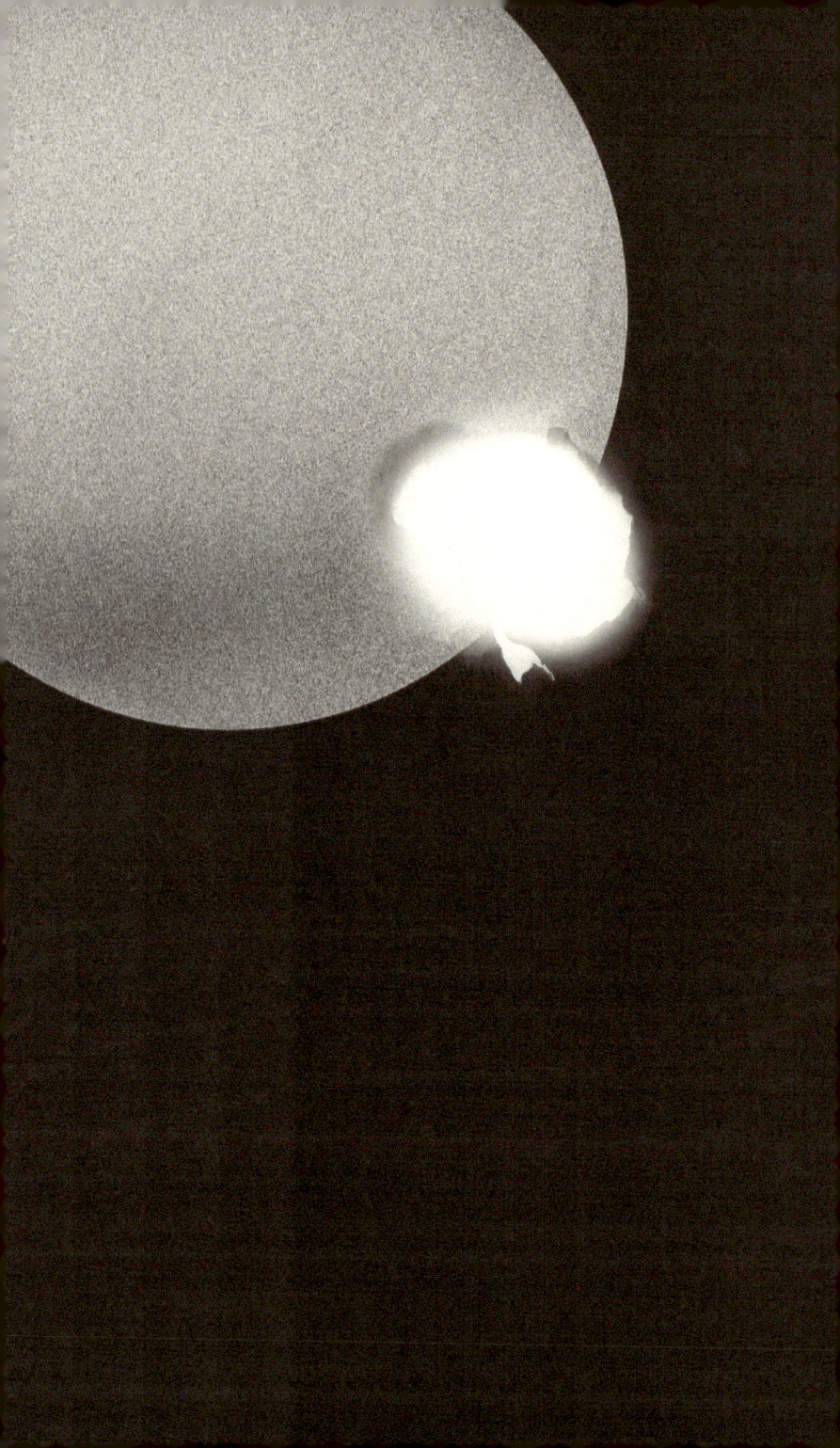

NEW MOON DARKNESS

New moon darkness all around my
head Everybody layin' down low
I'm tryin' to pick a spark from your black
moonlight I need someone who can show me where
to go Won't you please tell a body where to go

The skin of a snake and the skin of a
man are the only two that answer when I
call Bad luck's comin' from a mile away
But you never say who it's comin' for
So I just listen as it rolls right along

Destroy or deliver on that great skyline A body that you won't let go
I've been waitin' for that mornin' light so
long That I don't think it's ever gonna show
Won't you please let that mornin' light go

Shadows like mine were so easily made
You made them once and never will again
If only I could see with a heart like yours
I could finally make a body under-
stand A shadow can never be a man

New moon darkness all around my
head Everybody layin' down low
I'm tryin' to pick a spark from your black moon
light I need someone who can show me where
to go Won't you please tell a body where to go

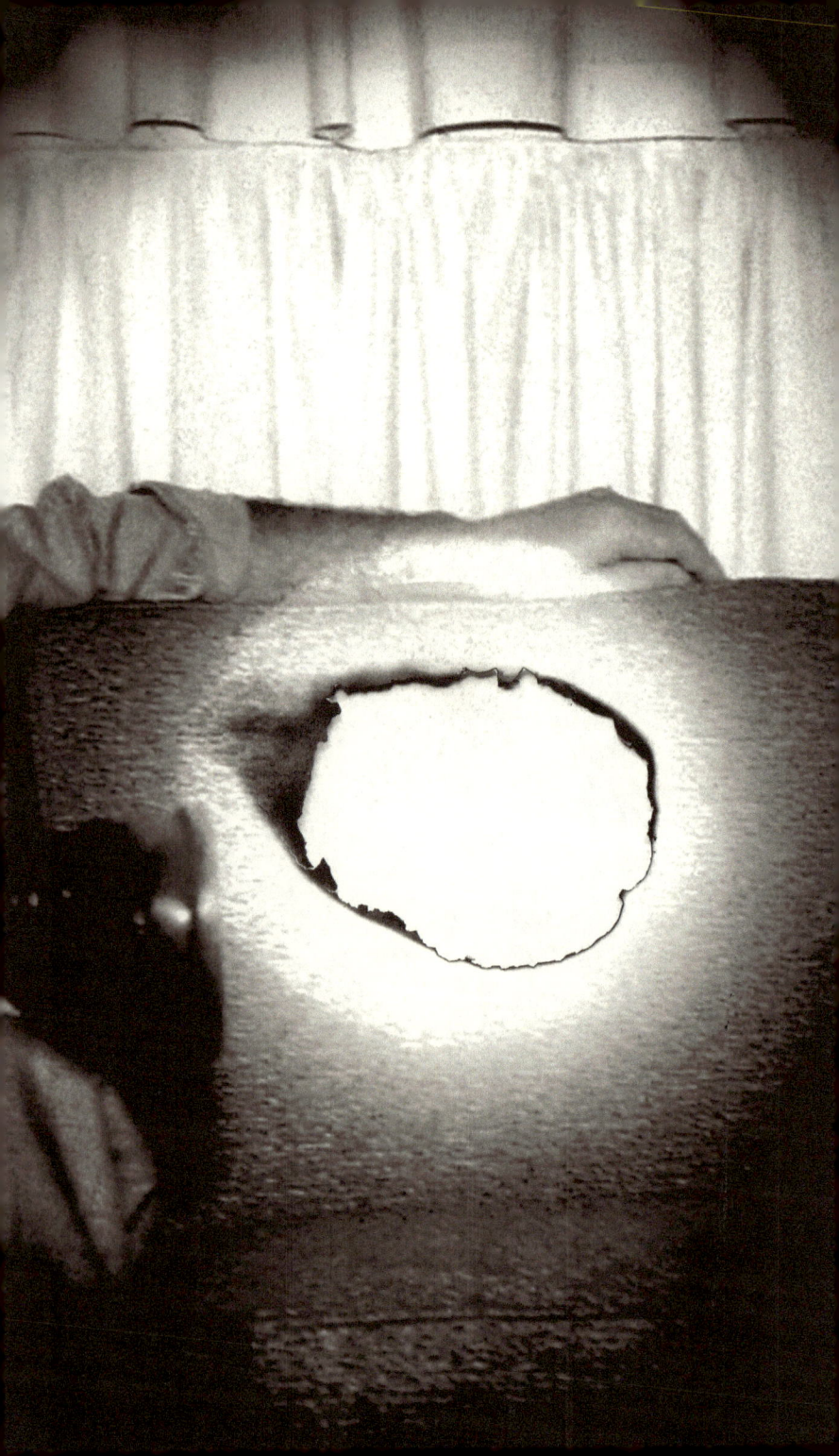

NEW MOON DARKNESS

Most days, Sadie rises early, just before dawn, sits on the edge of her twin bed and nestles her nine toes into the calico shag carpet that runs the length of the second floor. She rubs her red eyes and collects the constellation of crumpled tissues that have amassed around the bed, and drops them in the small birch-lined wastebasket by the door.

The bathroom is catty-corner to her mother's room at the end of the hall, but she doesn't look in her mother's room any-more, even though the door is always open. As she walks, she smiles at the cracked-knuckles sound the floor makes beneath the muffling shag. She rarely showers, just some cold water on the face and a few scissor snips to keep her brown bangs above the eyebrows and the rest off her shoulders, and sometimes a glance where the full length mirror once hung - Old habits.

Lately, however, she's added something new to her routine. It's her favorite part. She opens the medicine cabinet, looks inside, then closes it without removing any pill bottles. As the door shuts and her face flashes in the mirror, she laughs. She's got a great laugh. It's not raspy or phlegmy, but not a cackle either. It's more than air being pressed through a windpipe, there's a vocalization that goes with it. Almost like she sings a little when she laughs. Know that the pitch she laughs after doing her little medicine cabinet trick is slightly higher than usual, and it's been getting higher and longer by the day.

She leaves her flannel nightgown neatly folded on the bed before putting on her undergarments and picking out a pair of sweatpants and a sweatshirt. Today she's going with maroon on the top and bottom. It's her favorite combo.

The shag stops at the bottom of the stairs and gives way to cold hardwood in the living room and the dining room. In the kitchen, it's a lime green linoleum. It's the kind of house with waves and grooves worn into all of the surfaces.

There's an old meat grinder bolted to the kitchen counter that hasn't been used in decades, and a table covered in unopened soda cans, cereal, crackers, ding dongs, chips, and all manner of brightly colored packaging.

Most days, she would eat a cereal bar and have a soda, but today is special, and she's decided to bake herself a cake. It's going to take her a while to get all the pots and pans out of the oven and find the ingredients, so first she walks into the living room and flips on the monolithic tube television by the front door. It's a big wooden box with a curved grey screen.

On top, lots of picture frames are gathering dust. She presses rewind, then play on the VCR. Static wiggles by, then the voice of baseball play-by-play fills the air. It's the early innings from a lazy mid-summer afternoon game played some time ago. She loves the spaces the most, when you just hear a stadium of people idly passing time. A few shouts here and there, but mostly it's just the sound of people sitting outside. She especially loves this announcer because he leaves lots of space. Every now and then he gives the count or the score, but mostly, he just sits there like the rest of them. Very little happens in this game, which makes it her favorite. Sometimes, if she can't sleep, she'll lay on the couch with the game on. It helps, late at night, to just listen to all those people sit there. Today she needs to hear it way back in the kitchen, so she turns the volume way up. Now she can really hear those few yells in the background, and she decides to add in a few of her own. She urges the batter to, "Get a hit!", then yells a little louder for the pitcher to, "Get one by 'em!". She's having fun yelling at the TV, but the batter strikes out, and she remembers the cake.

By the time she's combined all the ingredients, the oven is ready and she slides her creation onto the metal rack wearing an oven mitt shaped like a fish. She closes the door and gets down on her hands and knees to look through the window. It's difficult getting back up, she has to use the kitchen chair.

Twenty-five to thirty minutes to kill, according to the box. She wonders if she needs to add more time to account for her additions. She decides ten extra minutes should do. Thirty-five to forty minutes gives her just enough time to do something she's been meaning to do for a while now.

She trudges back up the shag to the room at the top of the stairs. Stale air wafts out as she opens the door to the cramped space filled to the ceiling with relics. Behind a clothing form and some boxes, she sees them, black cases with SHAW stenciled in faded gold letters across the top. The small ones are easy to carry down, but the largest case has a broken leather strap, so she decides to roll it from the top, resulting in a big crash and some broken glass from the door at the bottom of the stairs. Don't worry, It's okay. The trap case, however, is completely unmoveable, so she carries each component down the stairs one at a time, careful not to cut her feet on any shards from the door.

The silver sparkle shines like they day they were made. She watched her brother set these things up hundreds of times, but she only has a vague notion of how these things fit together; the bass drum in the middle, snare drum off to one side, a few cymbals on stands. She decides to just rest the tom tom on the floor and forgo the high-hat. With the kick drum beater in one hand and a drumstick in the other, she plays.

At first it's tentative, a boom boom, crack. boom, boom, crack. Growing more comfortable, she tries Boom, crack, Boom, crack. She tries a cymbal, but it's not sitting on the stand quite right so it doesn't sizzle like she remembers. Back to the bass and the snare. Boom, Boom, Crack. Boom, Boom, Boom-Boom,

DESTROYER DELIVER

Crack. Yes, that's it. That's the one. Boom, Boom, Crack. Boom, Boom, Boom-Boom, Crack. She hits a little harder and a little faster now that she's got the groove. She looks at Eli's picture in the largest frame on top of the television. "Go, Man, Go!" She yells as she keeps her beat. She glances down at the baseball game, at those throngs of people, and she starts to play for them, louder and faster. She's sweating and running out of steam, but she's not stopping, she's hitting everything now, the tom, the cymbals, the rims, the skins, everything.

Go, man, go!

Boom, Boom, Crack, Boing, Snap, Ding, Boom, Boom, Boom-Boom, Crack, Boing, Crash, Crash, Boom-Boom, Crack, Boom, Crack, Boom, Crack, Boom, Crack, Boom, Crack, Boom.

Go, man, go!

Is that smoke?

Oh damn. Damn!

Don't worry, she's just going to cut off the burnt bits, it's fine.

Do those tubs of store bought icing expire? It looks ok. The cake isn't cool so the white goop is going to immediately slide off, but there's no time. Just slather on some more, then cover it with foil. You're late!

Wait. Wait! Just hold on a second. Let's all take a minute to regain our composure; It's dangerous out there.

The bus stop is right in front of Habig's on the corner. She has to walk over an uneven, weedy sidewalk to get there. At this time of morning, she doesn't see many people, just dogs behind chain-link fences. The people that she does see are pretty scary looking. Always young people. She wishes she would see an old person once in a while. Across from Habig's is a gas station, and catty-corner is a bakery that shut down a few years ago. When are they gonna put something new in there?

Here comes the bus. Do you have your money?

It's the same route every day, but she never recognizes the driver, not because she's senile, she's not, she has an excellent memory. Especially for things she cares about. No, it must be that they rotate the drivers for some reason.

Take the seat across from the rear door, it's far enough from the driver, but not so far back as to make you sick, or be dangerous. And be careful with the cake.

Today, the bus is empty as she stares at the skyline and tries to ignore the smell of the insulin factory. Look how bright everything is. There are some young people laughing on the sidewalk, and she wants to stop the bus and loiter with them, but you really can't do that because you took your sweet time this morning and you are late!

Look up ahead, a young woman is signaling to get on at Georgetown Rd. and she's got a small child. A boy. I hope they don't sit too close.

The woman pulls the boy on by the wrist and flings him down in the seats behind the driver that face out the side windows. It's pretty easy to tell she's mad because she's gesturing wildly. The boy is protesting with a strange sounding voice, and gesturing back. She realizes he must be deaf, and she finds herself watching their fingers flying angrily. The woman is really letting the boy have it, so the boy starts to cry and tries to look away, but she grabs him by the chin and snaps his head back around. He closes his eyes and that does it. She hauls off and smacks him across the face.

Go on, say something. Come on, Sadie, do something!

I guess you're going to just look away from the woman and the crying boy and ring the goddamn bell.

As the bus roars off, at the corner of Dock and Warren, she looks down the long avenue of shops. It's such a segregated town, all the rich people on this street and all the poor ones over there. She doesn't think anyone on this street even knows there's a factory one block over, but it doesn't really matter, does it? Maybe they all know. Every single last one of them. She feels like yelling down the block that there is a dirty, smelly, factory just one block away, but she doesn't.

She looks up at the gulls arcing through the sky above her and plays the drums in her mind. Isn't it so beautiful? She feels like she hasn't seen the sky or sunshine in a long, long time. And all that fear! Where did it go? Where did it go?! Where did what go? The cake? Oh yes, the cake is right here. Let's go, you're late.

DESTROYER DELIVER

She walks among them, cake in hand, but no one acknowledges her shadow as it creeps through the din of bodies, and weaves its way through the maze of machines. She watches the people mastering motions they'll make in their dreams, and listens to their shouted conversations breach the ocean of noise like surfacing whales.

She carefully sets the tin foil covered plate on the break room counter, then takes up her position on the floor.

The shop lights give her the complexion of a china doll as she guides pieces of quarter inch virgin teflon rod into the chasers and lets the machine spin, thread and cut the material. Speed is critical. Feed the rod too fast and the plastic melts; Too slow and the threads chip. She is adept at the motion. When she first started, she measured time by the clock, now she just lets it wash over her in great rolling waves.

Around lunchtime, Lila comes by clutching calipers and does a double-take when she looks down into the outtake bin at the bottom of the machine, and finds a handful of spent rod that looks like a jumble of burnt candles.

The mechanical roar turns beastly as Sadie presses another piece of rod violently into the chasers, and watches it melt, creating a small toxic cloud and a foul odor. Lila looks at her with a confused look on her face. Sadie smiles back.

"I brought a cake."

DESTROYER DELIVER

AXES AND AWLS

Brushed with fire and laid beside a brook
dry as a bone Those who knew me saw the
ashes billowing above the noise As a guide
to the land of ice to the land of stone
To the sound of the sway and the
thrust of the axes and awls Speak
softly and tell me I mattered once

I can hear the bells but I'm blind to the beat
I've been buried in your shadow so long How
many times can I open my mouth and hear
the words that you've already sung About a
heart in the land of ice, in the land of stone
About the sound of the sway and
the thrust of the axes and awls Speak
softly and tell me it's all been done

As the ice flows like blood from
the valley to my chest and lungs
It pulls my veins and hangs like a sickle
from the tip of my trembling tongue Where it
sways in the long slow day in a long slow arc
Watch it fall like the axe and the
awl with the quiet of a star Speak softly
and tell me you won't be far

AXES AND AWLS

The store is silent. The radio is just dead air, and Jerry's glad 'cause he doesn't wanna hear about that stuff anymore. Besides, he needs a little silence so he can think. Cary's on her way over to finish their argument face to face, and it's hard for him to focus when he can see that little baby bulge.

But, as he puts Kim Carnes into the new releases, the bell over the door jingles. It's that kid who's been coming around lately. He steals, but Jerry doesn't mind because he takes the stuff that no one ever buys; mostly cheap singles. The kid's not flipping through the bins though. He's pacing the aisles with his hands in his jacket pockets, and the bags under his eyes are deeper and darker than usual.

Neither acknowledges the other, they just go about their business. When the radio cuts in to provide more updates on the Lawton tragedy, Jerry turns it off.

As a new silence settles over them, the kid says, to no one in particular and without any prompting, "My mom wants me to join the Army." Then he looks at Jerry with an unsettling sincerity and asks, "Do you think I Should join the army?"

After a moment of contemplation, Jerry answers as

nonchalantly as possible, "Do you wanna be a soldier?"

"You know that kid they're talking about." The kid says, motioning toward the radio. "I knew him."

The way the kid cuts his hand through the air sends a shiver up Jerry's spine.

"Were you in the army?" The kid asks.

"No, but my old man was." Jerry says.

"The funny thing is," The kid continues, "I know I'd be a good soldier. A really good soldier. Maybe one of the best. I follow. I really follow. Just tell me what to do and I'll do it. And I can be pretty cold sometimes. Like when things get bad, I can turn off, and I bet that good soldiers can just shut down when they need to. No, I don't wanna be a soldier, but I'd be really good at it. Maybe that's why I don't wanna do it. But my uncle says that, when I'm not practicing to be a soldier, I'd have plenty of time to sit around and play my guitar."

The kid's keeping his right hand in his pocket, but he's running his left over the tops of the records and letting the plastic sleeves ripple beneath his palm as he speaks.

"I like your store man. I like just walking around in here. Do people always tell you to be careful? Everyone's always telling me to be careful. 'Be careful' is just a code for 'Be afraid' man. They're always telling me to 'Be afraid'. I got tired of being afraid, so I'm not afraid anymore."

The kid is getting agitated and he's sweating a little. "Are you afraid?" He asks Jerry. But before Jerry can respond, the kid interrupts, "That Lawton kid was afraid."

Out the front windows, everything is turning grey, and Jerry can see a man and a woman walking their bikes to the bike shop on the corner. He wants to pick up the phone and call Cary, but he knows she's already on her way over.

"Let me hear some music!" The kid yells. "Pick me out somethin' good, man!"

Jerry notices sweaty palm prints on the counter, as he steps behind the register.

"Maybe I should be a soldier like your old man!" The kid yells. "I'd be one of the best that ever lived! They'd build a statue of me and put it in front of the seven eleven on fifty-second street. I'd get every medal you can possibly get. I'd get a big golden bayonet to hang on my wall and my grandkids could sell it one day for a million bucks. Or I could use my guitar! I'll just strap my guitar to my rifle and take it into combat."

He keeps his right hand in his pocket while he stabs at the air with his left. "Come on, man! Let's hear some good goddamn music!"

As Jerry reaches for the closest record he can find, the kid yells, "NO! None a this crap! This is all a bunch a crap! Come on, man! Play me something good, goddamnit! Something I ain't heard already!"

With unsteady hands, Jerry pulls a slim box from a drawer beneath the register, and fumbles a reel-to-reel tape into the deck by the radio.

A loud hiss and the murmur of a small crowd come through the speakers. Someone says some indecipherable words into a microphone, and then the sound explodes with the Boom Boom Crack, Boom Boom Boom-Boom Crack of the drums followed by the bass and the guitar. The people in the room hoot and holler. At first It's difficult to make out, but after a few repetitions, the words to the chorus are clear:

She's the fire that lights my soul. She's the fire that lights my soul. She's the fire that lights my soul...

The kid's standing still with his eyes closed and neither says a word until the tape cuts out.

"Some old friends." Says Jerry.

The kid is shaking a little, and he doesn't open his eyes for a long time, but when he does, he snaps to attention with the precision of a military veteran, salutes with his left hand, and shuffles something from his right jacket pocket. Jerry instinctively squeezes his eyes shut, tightens every muscle in his body, flinches, and waits. But all he hears is the bell over the door, and when he opens his eyes, he sees the kid disappearing around the corner. In front of him, on the counter, is a hand-made cassette.

Across the parking lot, Cary is storming toward the door. She looks as young as the day they first met, and he can't remember what they were arguing about.

Before she enters, he drops John Hiatt on the turntable, scratches the needle to the beginning of 'The Night That Kenny Died' and turns the volume all the way up.

DESTROYER DELIVER

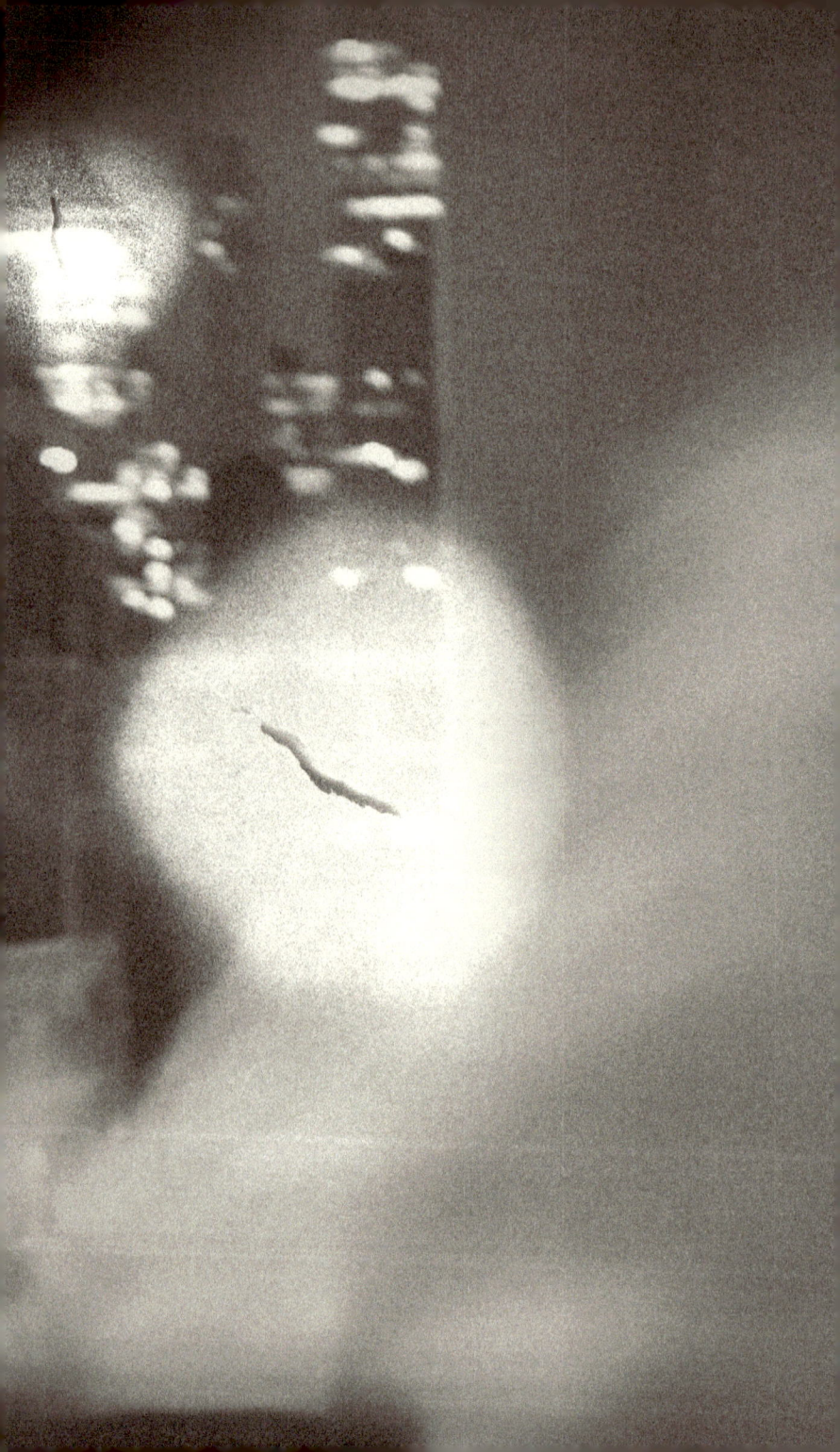

THE ARSONIST

I set my heart on fire on the wind-
ward blowin' side of this town
It set the night so bright you could
see the deepest scars in the ground And
when everyone comes for me
I'll just tell them that I needed
to see Your eyes, your eyes,
One last time.

And if the moon don't shine I can hide
beside the river till dawn But my heart still
rages you can see every shadow it throws And
when they put the last foot on the flame
They can put me out just the
same But tonight, but tonight
I'm alright.

And when the sun comes up I'll
be half way up the ridge
And if they haven't caught up I'll just
sit and watch the embers glow red
And if I make it to the top of the
hill, I'll just spread my arms and stand
so still In the light, in the light

And if I make it to the top of the hill, I'll
just spread my arms and stand so still

THE ARSONIST

Welcome to the Sunsphere. The Sun is the perfect sphere of hot plasma at the center of our Solar System. It is the most important source of energy for life on Earth.

No matter what the woman on the television monitor says, she still can't help seeing that poor thing laid bare on a dimly lit stage, with its eyes looking at her, pleading.

At the end of the short video, she's ushered into the main observation area. Considering she's in a room made entirely of windows, it's not very bright. She expected to step out of the elevator into a glowing blaze, but the space is muted and grey.

She has no desire to stand at the glass and look out, so she walks to a small plastic bench at the far side of the elevator shaft and sits down. Hanging before her, almost at eye-level, is an orange banner that reads, "The 1982 World's Fair: Energy Turns the World!"

As she leans back against the wall and lets her muscles relax in the cool air, she tries to shake the mummy unveiling she saw at the Peruvian exhibit, but it just keeps playing over in her mind.

From the back of the room, the eyes of the child didn't look like empty sockets. They looked full and open.

She wonders who did the wrapping. Who pulled on the strands

and held them tight as they were neatly tucked under the limbs then passed from one pair of hands to the next. Who carefully kept pressure on the folds so the strands wouldn't unfurl. Did someone sing as they covered the eyes? She wonders how many times the strands came undone before they finally got it right.

All those people clicking away with their cameras; It was a carnival sideshow. She feels ashamed of herself for bearing witness.

Throughout the entire presentation, they never referred to the mummy as someone's child. "Oh Francis. It was horrible." She says quietly to herself.

She thought about saying something, or doing something, but she did nothing. She just stood there with the rest of them until, in a matter of minutes, all of the strands had been unfurled.

Around her, families are coming and going, couples are holding hands, and a few loners are staring out at the fair. She wants to sleep, but in public she can't help but jolt herself awake, so she imagines her husband singing. It's something she likes to do whenever she has to kill time.

Down said the owl with his head all white Lonesome day and lonesome night First to the left then to the right This old mill grinds day and night

She can still hear the woman from the television monitor in the small room by the elevators.

The sun's atmosphere has three layers. The visible light we see on Earth comes from the lowest layer, The Photosphere.

Eventually, she gets up, walks to the railing of the giant windows, and presses her forehead against the glass.

Below are all manner of people bustling about from pavilion to pavilion, but she doesn't like this place, and she doesn't want to see these people anymore, so she looks out, beyond the fair, beyond the cars streaming like rivers, beyond the low buildings of the surrounding city, beyond it all.

She thinks that if she can just look far enough, she'll see Francis out there, sitting beneath a white-headed owl, trying so hard to wrap their boy. But he's alone, and those long, red ribbons just keep unspooling.

The Chromosphere emits a reddish glow, but it can only be seen during a total solar eclipse.

She closes her eyes and wishes she were in the middle of the real sun. She would absorb all of its massive energy and explode outward, wrapping herself around them so tightly that no one would ever be able to unfurl the strands.

Why the Corona is the hottest of the three layers, despite being the furthest from the sun's core, remains a mystery.

When she opens her eyes, a halo of warm breath is spread on the cool glass before her, and as she backs away, it evaporates from the outside in, revealing the sun in the distance, slowly falling behind the faraway hills. In the reflection of the glass, she can see Belle and the kids, Sadie, and Cary stepping out of the elevator.

She's happy to see her children and her grandchildren, but she doesn't turn away from the sun. She looks to the horizon, where it's hiding like a coward.

In that moment, the fleeting light catches her just so, and she smiles. She is a universe, a mass of churning stars, a cosmic fire.

DESTROYER DELIVER

HEARTS LIKE OURS

Hearts like ours are comin' round the
bend Bare as stone and bold as bones and
sin You keep your eyes on the sky
And I'll keep mine on the ships rollin' in.

Any day they're gonna drop like bombs (You
better cover up your eyes) Scattered bursts of bitter
verse and song (You better cover up your ears)
You find a place to hide
And I'll stay here and sing along

Hearts like ours Are fallin'
like stars Hearts like ours

Rusted out and trapped like little birds (Here come
our friends to set us free) Singin' songs of fire with
paper words (And though we shout they cannot see)
We'll sit and bide our time watchin'
the verses rise and burn

Oh my friend it's time to sing along
(but we've been singing all along)
When they hear our harmony they'll fall
(Oh can't you hear us sing this song)
You just turn away, raise a glass and say, "So
long." (So long to you, my friend, so long!)

Oh my friend They're listening Oh my friend

Hearts like ours are comin' round the bend
(Hearts like ours are fallin' down like stars) Hearts
like ours are comin' round the bend (Hearts like
ours are burning in the fire) Hearts like ours are
comin' round the bend (Hearts like ours are fallin'
down like stars) Hearts like ours are comin' round
the bend (Hearts like ours are burning in the fire)

HEARTS LIKE OURS

"Don't worry. It's gonna be ok."

But she's not quite sure what the hell to do. Usually there's lots of cops around here, but right now she doesn't see any. And shit – She's a little messed up. Talking to cops is probably a bad idea. There's the hotdog stand across the way, but she's not takin' the kid over there, no way. That guy's a creep.

Wait. Just wait here. The parents will come around. So she gives the kid one of those pens that when you tip it over it makes a little racecar go from one side to the other to calm him down, then she takes him by the hand and guides him back around through the little opening at the back of the stand and sits him down on a folding chair beneath the inflatable flamingos.

"What's your name?" She asks, but the little boy just has his head down and he's slowly tipping the pen back and forth. She asks a few times, but gets nowhere. Finally, she taps his knee and he looks up at her with red eyes and snot-smeared cheeks. She asks again and this time he opens his mouth, but an unintelligible sound comes out. He's got a big string of drool that's drooping from his lip and hanging off his chin. Shit. She grabs a receipt, scribbles "What's your name?" on the back and hands it to him, but he just looks at it. Shit. She motions for him to, go on, write something, but all he does is scribble big circles. Shit. She takes the pen back and draws a big stick figure. Beneath it she writes, in all caps, CARY. Then she kneels down and says it real slowly for him. He opens his mouth. More drool spills out as he says "Airy". That's good. That's okay. Then he squeals a lump of vowel sounds. He's telling her his name, but she can't understand, so she just nods. Shit.

A languorous voice cuts through the air, "Please clear the pit lane because we are back to green. Green on the racecourse."

She gets up and looks around Lot 4 again. Still no sign of anyone in distress. The kid is getting a little antsy, so she takes down a red Matchbox car and gives it to him. He runs it around the tufts of grass on the floor of the stand and makes some little noises. While he's pushing the car back and forth, she slips a Rick Mears T-shirt over his head and onto his skinny little body. It's too big, and he squirms a little, but he leaves it on.

Wait. Shit. They can't stay here. She can't let Southmain find the kid here. Damnit. There's a payphone at Georgetown and McCray. He'll be pissed if she leaves the stand, but he'll be more pissed if he finds the kid here.

She'll call Jerry. Jerry'll know what to do. But he's at the store. What the hell is that number?

Maybe she should just stand the kid a little ways off in the lot, keep an eye on him, and hope someone else comes along? She looks down at his little towhead. Damnit. She can't do that.

A car roars past, but the little boy never flinches, he just keeps pushing the Matchbox car around in the dirt.

"Car number 84 on the track. J.R. possibly getting ready for an attempt." eases lazily from the PA.

She rummages through her bag and tries to give the kid some gum, but he doesn't want it. She gets up and looks around the lot again. There's a guy trying to get a cooler in his trunk across the way, but he's so drunk he nearly falls over backwards in the process.

She looks down at the boy again. Shit.

The car rushes by, "197.062 for the 84 car. Not good enough

if he wants to bump his way into the field."

Mom. She'll know what to do. Maybe she can get Sadie to drive over. Or Belle, but she really doesn't wanna call Belle unless she absolutely has to.

She looks in her bag. Shit. She grabs a wad of cash from the register, scribbles a note and ties the plastic flaps across the front.

As they walk south on Georgetown, she's scanning faces. Everyone on this street seems to be drunk, or sunburned, or both. All the women have knotted shirts over bare midriffs and sweaty foreheads. The men are cat calling. She looks around at all the parked cars. It feels like there's some shady stuff going on in most of them. The further south they go the more distorted everything gets.

After a while, the kid starts pulling at her hand, and Cary guesses he's getting hungry, so they stop in front of a white cotton candy trailer covered in incandescent bulbs and wait for the lady to take their order. She's older, about Mom's age, with big bushy brown hair. Cary feels relieved. She's gonna tell this lady what's going on and get this thing off her shoulders, but before she can, the woman leans out the window and tells Cary to stop her kid from slobbering all over the counter. She's got an angry look in her eye like she's tired of dealing with snot-nosed kids all day. Shit. Cary buys a bag and they leave.

It must've been a while since the little boy ate 'cause he shoves big handfuls of cotton candy into his mouth as they walk.

At 25th street they pass a woman selling airbrushed mirrors.

"Got a nice Tom Sneva mirror over here. It'd look good in that little man's room."

She's got a raspy voice and she's missing some teeth, but it's more about the way she says "little man" though. No, she's not the one.

At 24th street, they pass a man in a Marines uniform. He doesn't look too drunk.

"Excuse me, sir." She says.

But he doesn't say anything back, just stares in her eyes. She

DESTROYER DELIVER

can tell he's seen some shit. "Sorry." She says, and she hustles them away.

Finally, up ahead, at McCray, she sees the payphone.

As they stand there in the little box, she starts to lift the receiver, but. Shit. Mom is gonna know she's messed up the second she opens her mouth. Damnit. She's gotta call Belle. But when she dials, it just rings and rings and rings. Damn. She racks her brain trying to remember the number at the store. She wishes she weren't messed up. Maybe if she weren't messed up right now she could get a hold of Jerry, but she can't remember the number at the store. She's gonna have to call Mom and hope Sadie picks up, but when she dials, it just rings and rings and rings.

Louisville. They're all in Louisville visiting Agnes. As she hangs up the receiver, the little boy throws up all over the booth. Shit.

"J.R. turning some good laps." Says the voice of the public address system.

Beneath the overcast, late-afternoon sky, she wipes at the boys vomit covered shins with the bottom edge of the Rick Mears shirt.

"Yellow. Yellow. Debris on the racecourse."

She loves how the announcer says the word "debris" like "day-bree".

That voice. She's being hearing that voice her whole life. Sometimes, on really still days, she can hear the echoes of that voice from their backyard.

And then it hits her. The P.A.

She pulls out the wad of crumpled cash from her shorts pocket and counts it. She's got just enough.

Inside, the sound is different. It's louder, and you can follow the roar of the cars all the way around. But right now, all she hears is "The Stars and Stripes Forever" blaring around the track through hundreds of horn shaped speakers that were manufactured sometime in the 1940's. She gets a lump in her throat when the march comes to a hard stop and echoes in waves around the two and a half mile oval. Even though she's worked at Southmain's stand for a while now, she hasn't stepped foot inside the speedway since she was little.

Before they can do anything, though, she's gotta get this poor kid something to eat, so with her last few dollars she buys him a hot dog and a coke, and they sit down to take a rest for a while in the lower part of the tower terrace.

The place looks more massive from the inside. She looks down the pit lane at the scattered bodies. It's mostly empty except for a hive of activity in a few of the boxes. She figures one of them must be J.R.'s pitbox. They've been talking about him all morning, how he's trying to make a last ditch effort to get in. She's never been a big fan of his, but she's pulling for him.

Across the way, along the outside wall at the exit of turn four she can see some big black tire marks from where someone hit the wall earlier in the day. She doesn't like the wrecks, and she doesn't like the people who do. Some people will openly say that they like the wrecks, and she cringes a little when she hears that. They haven't heard as many as she has. She knows when they're minor, and she knows when they're fatal. All from the sound.

As the boy eats, she swabs at his chin and wipes his mouth. He's got a real sweet nature about him. Every now and then he points at something and implores her to look, but she doesn't quite know what she's supposed to see, so she just nods in as cheerful a way as she can muster. He doesn't seem to be afraid. In fact, he seems to be having fun, but just as Cary finds herself hoping for a green light, she remembers what they came in here for.

The P.A. announcer must sit at the top of the pagoda, which is the squat tower directly across from the flag stand at the start/finish line, so they head in that direction.

The areas around the garages and the pits are always busy, even on the last weekend of qualifying, so the crowd is thick as they approach gasoline alley. A yellow-shirt starts blowing his whistle and the foot traffic comes to a halt. She pushes them forward to the edge of the crowd just as the 84 car is being towed back out of the garage and into the pits. Some of

DESTROYER DELIVER

the people yell out to J.R. as he saunters by, deep in conversation with someone. He looks wholesome yet weather-beaten, flashing his pearly white smile and waving his driving gloves at the crowd.

The yellow-shirts. Why didn't she think of that before? I'll talk to one of the yellow-shirts. They'll be able to help. But when she looks down, the little boy is gone and Cary's heart stops beating. She's frantic. She spins around and looks at the camera clad tourists, the sponsor clad race teams, the yellow clad yellow-shirts. He's nowhere. But as she's about to scream, she sees him, bent down in the dirt, picking up the tab from a beer can. She knocks it out of his hand and tells him not to do that.

Once the car has passed, and the crowd is allowed to cross, she approaches the yellow-shirt with the whistle.

"Sir?" She says.

"Yes, mam?"

"I've got a lost little boy here."

"Yes, mam, you see that building right down there? That's the sheriff's office, just take him down there."

Before she can respond, the man starts blowing his whistle again.

Shit. She doesn't wanna go in the sheriff's office. Not like this.

"Ok." She says to the boy very slowly so he can see her mouth. "You walk in that door and tell them you're lost. Ok?" But the boy is just looking at her with wide eyes. "Just go in there." And she points to the door, but he grabs her outstretched hand. Shit.

"Wait, Sir!" And she calls back after the yellow-shirt. "How do we get into the Pagoda?"

"You gotta badge?" He asks.

"No."

"Then you can't go in there." And he starts blowing again.

The whistle is piercing and the crowd is bustling, loud, and hot. She's feeling a little sick, and she's mad at herself for being messed up, and mad at this kid because he just keeps drooling.

She needs to get away from this crowd for a second. She just needs to figure out what the hell is going on.

She looks up to see, in front of them, the massive grandstand in turn one, and remembers Dad always saying, "Best view in the house." That's where they need to go. They need to get above it all and just figure this out once and for all, so she grabs the kid by the hand and pulls him toward the tunnel under turn one.

When they get to the other side, they've got little chains across the aisles to grandstand E, but they're easy to slide under. It's a lot of stairs all the way up to the penthouse and she ends up carrying the boy on her back most of the way. He laughs as they bob up the long steps, and she can feel his saliva running down her shirt.

The view is astounding, They can see almost all the way around the track from up here. She scans the sea of green seats and there's no one around. It's just them up there.

"We've got a qualifier!" Says the voice over the P.A.

Below, a car sputters to life and revs its engine as it pulls down the pit lane and enters the track. She listens to the engine struggle through the low gears until it finds its footing and the car starts to build speed exiting turn two.

Seeing the car from up here, so small against the massive structure, she is overcome with admiration. God, she hopes he can make it in.

She listens to the high pitched whine of the engine at full speed now as it makes its way out of four and heads to the line.

"And heeee's on it. Let's hear it for J.R."

She gives him the racecar cheer, which is simply to wave your hands in the air because the drivers can't hear anything.

He's really moving. After he crosses the line on his first lap, she leans forward in her seat and waits for the call.

"It's a fast one! 203.156!"

A smattering of applause goes up from the diehards who are still scattered around the oval, but there's a problem. Smoke. It's starting to stream out of the engine in little grey wisps, but he's not stopping, he's keeping it together somehow.

Lap two and three are slower, much slower, but he's still got

DESTROYER DELIVER

a chance, if he can just bring it home. She's on her feet now, clutching her hands together at her chest as the red, white, and blue race helmet with the big white star on top flashes beneath her. Just keep going, she thinks.

"All four tires below the white line in turn one as he inches close to the wall in the short chute! Out of turn two and so close to the wall again as he propels himself down the backstretch! Into turn three with two tires below the stripe as he makes his way into the north end of the track! He lifts a little going through four, but he's really flying as he scrapes the wall on his way back to the stripe!"

As the car shoots out of the corner and ducks down to the inside line, she sees the little boy next to her. He's jumping up and down with tears in his eyes and drool flying from his chin. She puts her hands on his shoulders and thinks about being here with Eli and Dad, and how, after a day of running around the infield grass, Eli would set her down in the backseat of the stationwagon and close the heavy door. She remembers that moment of being alone in there, and hearing their voices outside, but not being able to make out the words.

"And he crosses the line!"

They're both jumping now, and as the dark blue car passes beneath them, she teaches him how to wave his hands in a driver's cheer, and they both do it together, they silently wave their hands in the air.

And then they wait.

They wait for the voice to tell them if it was good enough.

RIGHT AS RAIN

I saw you prayin' by the courthouse steps
to be right as rain, to be right as rain
You know this place in its full moon bliss is
gonna make you pay, it's gonna make you pay
Then you looked up at the night and shouted
"Hallelujah I can do it if I make it back home."

I saw a woman in a river garden she was
chilled to the bone she was chilled to the bone
She put her hand on my shoulder and said, "We
can make a good home, we can make a good home."
Then I looked out at the river and shouted
"Hallelujah I don't need you,
you can leave me alone."

I spend my time in a photograph feelin'
right as rain, feelin' right as rain
You know this town in its full moon bliss is
gonna take it away, it's gonna take it away
Then I looked up at the city and shouted,
"Hallelujah you can have it I
don't need it no more."

RIGHT AS RAIN

And like clockwork, the gulls are gathering along the track in center. Boy it'll be slim pickins today.

Nieves steps out.

Look at that kid out there.

He's got the entire right field bleachers to himself. Lou, can we get a shot of that kid?

All those empty blue seats and then...there he is.

You know, Lou, that kid is the spitting image of me when I was that age.

And the 2-1.

That's low for ball three.

Makes me lonesome to see that kid sittin' out there all by himself.

Wickman's got a good one goin'. Only given up three hits through eight and two thirds. That slider is really workin' for 'em today.

He hasn't gotten much offense, but he hasn't needed it.

What do I know? Maybe he likes watchin' the game from way out there, away from everyone else. He must.

All I know is that when I was that kid's age, I was already

married and calling games in the Southern Association.

God, when did I call my first AAA game? '45? I woulda been 20 years old.

Geez, 1945.

This place woulda been a lot fuller then, I can tell ya that much.

Wickman deals.

Just caught the outside corner. Nieves doesn't like it, and he's letting the home plate umpire know about it.

I remember listening to the late, great Bill Slater call that '45 series like it was yesterday.

Lulu and I in Atlanta, sitting in our little kitchen. God it was hot down there.

The Cubs ran away with game 1, but Hank Greenberg hit one a country mile in game 2 and boy that really turned it all around.

Lou, can you put that kid back on the screen?

Look at him. Doesn't have a clue.

Wickman takes his time coming set.

And the pitch.

He walked him.

So with two out here in the ninth, the Tigers have the tying run aboard.

Looks like Phil Garner is gonna pinch hit for Hunter.

I wonder what ever happened to Bill Slater.

The last time I heard his voice was. God, probably his call of the '47 Indy 500. Mauri Rose won it that year. What a driver.

Shorty Cantlon died in that terrible wreck.

They just left his car crunched against the wall for the rest of the race. Can't imagine havin' to pass that mangled car every lap.

Speaking of Indianapolis, Garner is gonna bring up Tines.

It says here Tines hit .285 over seven seasons in Indianapolis. Came over from the Red's in that Torres deal.

Wow. Seven seasons. That's a long time in the minors. Let's see if he can get something going.

Wickman looks in.

And Tines fouls it back.

I hope they sprinkled Bill's ashes over a microphone somewhere. God he was good.

Matheny heads out to the mound to make sure everyone's on the same page.

When I die, don't let them sprinkle my ashes over water. Especially not the ocean. Make sure it's dry ground. The thought of drifting way down to the bottom and being in the deep dark...

Lulu's back in West Virginia.

Took some of her to a little park in Atlanta.

Mostly she's in the garden.

Here comes Barnett to break up the party.

Ya know, when I think about the way it was then and the way it is now. Truthfully, just between you and me, it's all the same. Some of you old timers out there might know what I'm talking about.

Here's the 0-1.

In the dirt for ball one.

I can see a few umbrellas opening up beneath me here in the booth.

Got married at a little courthouse in the middle a nowhere.

We were on the road for an away game and we just decided to hell with it. Let's do it now.

The funny thing is, we really got into it on the drive to the next game, and Lulu chucked her wedding ring right out the car window!

We never did find it.

She didn't wear one after that, but I didn't care. Didn't need to.

Wickman comes set. And delivers.

Oh boy, how'd he lay off that breaking ball? Two balls and a strike.

That kid out there with the seagulls is stayin' put.

Look at all those scavengers out there. There must be two dozen of em fightin' over a hotdog bun.

Boy, that kid is soaked through, but he's not movin'.

DESTROYER DELIVER

It looks like he's praying.

Is that what it looks like to you, lou?

I think that kid is kneeling out there by himself in the rain, praying.

Come on, Tines. Get a hit for us.

The pitch.

Just misses the bottom of the zone, 3-1

I haven't prayed in a long time.

Jaha is holding Nieves on, so there's a big hole on the right side of the infield if he can just get the bat on the ball.

The offering.

Oh. Tines had a good one there and he knows it. Got a little underneath it and fouled it straight back.

Full count.

They're down to their last strike.

You hear that?

It's that kid out in right.

Boy he's really cheering like crazy all of a sudden. You can probably hear him through my microphone he's yellin' so loud.

He's jumpin' up and down. Lou? You gotta shot of him? Look at that.

He's yellin' his head off.

Atta boy. Don't give up yet.

Get some a these people to wake up and listen.

God, I hope Tines can get a hit for us.

Come on, folks, do you hear that?

Listen to that kid. He's really trying to wake everyone up.

He doesn't wanna see this thing come to an end.

Don't look away. Listen to him! He's trying! He's really trying to do his best out there!

We've gotta keep this thing alive!

There's still time!

(pause)

For now the winter is past

The rain has ended and gone away

The blossoms appear in the countryside

The time of singing has come

And the turtledove's cooing is heard in our land
Amen

DESTROYER DELIVER

AWAY, MY DESTROYER

Away with you my great destroyer
It's time to leave you again
I want a heart like the others
Out on the new wasteland

They'll find your blood in the
ocean They'll find your bones in the
sand After they put you together
Please come and see me again

Where I go is where you'll be On the
plains or on the sea Even in a memory
You can come and destroy me

Away with you my great destroyer
It's time to leave you again
I want a heart like the others
Out on the new wasteland

Away with you my great
destroyer I know I'll see you again
Out on the great black highway
Headin' back from the old wasteland

We'll dance, old alibi
Clap hands, sing by the fire
Shoot words, cover our eyes
In the morning we'll say good bye

Where I go is where you'll
be Singin' out a melody
Even in a memory
You can come and destroy me

So away with you my great
destroyer I know I'll see you again
Out on the great black highway
Headin' back from the old wasteland

Away with you my great destroyer
Our time has come to an end
I hope one day you will find
me Out on the new wasteland

I'll leave my blood in the ocean
I'll lay my bones in the sand

After you pull me together
Please come and see me again

Where I go is where you'll be On the
plains or on the sea Even in a memory
You can come and destroy me

Away with you my great destroyer
Our time has come to an end
I hope one day you will find
me Out on the new wasteland

AWAY, MY DESTROYER

Sorry about that! Not tryin' to ignore you! What?! Sorry! What?! Gotta speak up! You liked the set?! Oh thanks man!

Hey Ronny! Where's my high-hat stand?! Great! Thanks Brother!

Here! You mind takin' these! I'll get this goddamn trap! Why'd I have to be a drummer! Am I right?! I shoulda been a flute player or somethin'!

Oh it feels good to get outta there. You can just throw that anywhere in the backseat. Thanks, man. You gotta light?

No, it's a Ludwig. I used to play a Slingerland, but I couldn't make it sound the way I wanted, so I sold it. I think the Ludwig sounds outta sight. And that silver sparkle, man. I thought about the blue, but the silver is far out. Didn't it look good under the lights? Even in a tiny place like this, it really shines up there. It looks like I'm playin' on the milky way or somethin'.

Nice to meet you, too. I'm Eli. You in one of the other bands? You came out just for our set? Far out.

Thanks, we're starting to find it. Took us a while, but it's locking. We're gonna cut a record soon. Ronny's cousin knows a place where we can lay somethin' down - Just gotta get the money together.

'Light My Soul'? Herb wrote that one, but I helped out on the chorus a little. Herbie wanted it to go, (sung) "She's the fire that lights my soul", and he was going way up like that on the "soul" part, but I said, "try it coming back down on 'soul' like this, (sung) "She's the fire that lights my...soul." They all dug it, so we kept it that way, but now Herb wants Ronny to sing, *It's the fire that lights my soul*, 'cause his girlfriend just dumped him. The rest of the song doesn't make any sense if you do that though, ya know? The whole thing's a mess. Oh, hold on a sec.

Bellie! You came!

What'd you think of the set?

Rave On? Really? I thought that was our worst one – Joe and John screwed up the harmonies!

Where's Cary? Did she come?

Aw hell. Well Jerry brought his reel-to-reel, so I'll play her the tape.

Listen, tell Sadie and them that I'll meet 'em at the diner as soon as we get paid.

You gonna join us? Why not, you got stories to scribble down?

Hey, I told Mom and Dad I'd go to church with 'em tomorrow, so try to get up before we leave – I wanna hear about Biloxi. And I wanna see a picture of you in uniform!

Alright Bellie. Be careful, sis.

Sorry about that. You got sisters?

It's a trip. I got three of 'em.

No, I'm the only musician in the family. Well, I guess I should say I'm the only one who plays in public. Sadie's got a great voice but, I don't know, she just won't sing in front of people. I hear her through the walls sometimes. She sings 'Ticket to Ride' and I think, man, why won't she do that for a room full of people! And, just between us, she writes killer songs too. Listen, if you meet her, don't tell her I said that, 'cause she doesn't know that I know. I was leaving for work one day and I just saw her sitting there on the floor through the crack in the door, and she was writing with her eyes closed.

Yeah, man. With her eyes closed! She was sitting with her

DESTROYER DELIVER

back against the bed-frame and holding a notepad on her lap. She was really into it, and I felt strange watchin' her, but it was hard not to. She just kept writin' and writin'. Pages and pages of stuff, and she never opened her eyes. Listen, I'm not a snooper, but I had to sneak in there when she was gone and take a look - It was really outta sight stuff. Pages of songs. But they weren't about boyfriends and girlfriends, that kinda stuff. They were about love, but not that kinda love. I mean, I could get what she was sayin', even though they were about really strange things, ya know? Big things and small things at the same time. It's hard to explain, man. And the really crazy thing is, I could hear the music. I mean, there was no music, just the words, but I could hear the melodies and stuff. It was really outta sight.

Other than that, my old man'll go out to the garage and bang on my kit sometimes, but he doesn't really know what he's doin'. I should go out there and show him how to keep a beat to one a those country songs he likes, but I just sit on the back porch and listen.

I love playin' in that garage. It sounds great in there - All those tools, and bikes, and rakes and stuff, man. All that metal must give the sound and extra zing or somethin'. At first I hated playin' in there cause it's really dank and there's spiders everywhere, but after I cleaned it out I started to dig it. I still get spiders crawlin' across my kit sometimes, but if I see one I let it crawl onto the tip of my stick then I fling it outside. I hate smashin' 'em into the heads. On nights like tonight man, when there's a nice smell in the air, and it's not too hot or too cold, I can just sit out there all night.

Can I tell you somethin'? Last night, when I was in the garage, I saw someone out by the tomato plants, sittin' on the fence and smokin' a cigarette - Just a shadow and an orange dot. I thought about goin' out and talkin' to 'em, seein' who it was, but I got the feelin' that, whoever it was, they just wanted to sit and listen for a while, so I played and played. I played for hours. When I came out, they weren't there anymore. It was strange, man.

DESTROYER DELIVER

You wanna bum a smoke?

Hey, you know the song, 'Tomorrow Never Knows'? I play till my hands bleed, man, and I can't make it sound like Ringo. Did you know the Beatles played in this town a few years ago? I couldn't get within a mile of the Coliseum, but Sadie snuck in and saw the whole show! She didn't hear one note, but she didn't care. Just to see em in person was...well, it was somethin'.

You should stick around and check out this next band 'cause they have a killer lead guitar player, and their songs are really outta sight. They just got back from Los Angeles. They played on the strip! Just between you and me though, I think we can be better than them. We just gotta start makin' enough from shows to quit our jobs so we can practice more. That and stay out of the draft, man.

You know what some friends of mine just did? After the combine went through, they went out into a big open corn field and one of em stood at one end and one of em stood at the other and they each had .22's and they took turns shootin' right over the other one's head. And they said it wasn't so bad.

Aw hell. You see this guy comin' up? He's out here every night, man. I feel bad for em. He's just gettin' picked on by the cops all the time. Our first show here, I was packin' up and he walked over to panhandle and some cop came up and grabbed him by the collar and threw him into the paddy wagon. A real drag, man. I've talked to him since then and he ain't a bad guy. Just a drunk.

Hey man, you need a dollar? Here you go, man. No sweat. You take it easy. And be careful, Ok? you gotta be careful.

What time is it?

Oh hell, I gotta go meet Sadie and them.

Hey Johnny! Where's Jerry? I gotta take off man.

Just give me my cut next weekend, and tell Jerry that's too many bands on the bill for next Friday.

Yeah yeah. Thanks Johnny. I'll see ya Wednesday.

Sadies tunes? Well, I gotta get goin', but, yeah, I'll tell you about one I guess, but if she ever finds out I told you...Let me see, there's a bunch, but my favorite is about this bird that circles a place that's way out in the water and it's surrounded by all these buoys. There's this man and this woman...

That's the melody I heard in my head, too...

Ya know, I go to church with my folks on Sunday, and most of the time I'm so tired I sleep right through the service, but last weekend, just as I was driftin' off, the priest said the words, "Destroyer Deliver", and all of a sudden, a bird flew right through the rafters of St. Anthony's. It looked just how I picture that bird from Sadie's tune. I watched it circle a few times before it set down on one of the beams. As I sat there lookin' up at it, those words, 'Destroyer Deliver', started playin' around in my head, and I couldn't figure out if it was "Destroyer Deliver" or "Destroy or Deliver". I mean, I couldn't figure out if it was a command or a choice. I...I dunno.

Here, take another smoke for the road.

Man, look at that night sky - Never seen so many stars.

Yeah, you're right. It does look like my kit.

DESTROYER DELIVER

EPILOGUE

The storm has come and gone.

From the crest of each swell, Tau watches the lone body, still moving through the sea with great power, grow smaller and smaller, until it is swallowed up by the golden light of the falling star.

Above him, the great bird circles, letting a few worn feathers fall upon the water below.

☐ **DESCENDER by Descender** (ALR 001)
6 song debut EP. Available formats: Digipak CD, digital / streaming
90's Influenced post-hardcore. RIYL: Snapcase, Helmet, Quicksand

"Angularly aggressive hardcore that takes an abrasive shape on purpose." – CMJ

☐ **AND SO WE MARCHED by Descender** (ALR 002)
4 song EP. Available formats: Printed book, digital / streaming
90's Influenced post-hardcore. RIYL: Snapcase, Helmet, Quicksand

"...a 21st Century compliant post-hardcore band that was raised on metal and got dosed with a tab of AmRep..." – Jaded Scenster

☐ **TAKING DRUGS TO MAKE MUSIC TO SELL CARS TO**
by Human Highlight Reel (ALR 003)
4 song debut EP. Available formats: Vinyl record, printed book, digital / streaming
Instrumental post-rock. RIYL: Maserati, June of 44, Russian Circles

"Aces instrumental post rock. Think Russian Circles or perhaps a more metal Seam..." – Jaded Scenster

☐ **JUDGE by Vagina Panther** (ALR 004)
5 song EP. Available formats: Printed book, digital / streaming
Heavy female-fronted garage rock. RIYL: QOTSA, Cheeseburger, Fu Manchu, Stooges

"Vagina Panther rocks." – Billboard

☐ **BLACK BLACK BLACK by Black Black Black** (ALR 005)
12 song debut LP. Available formats: Vinyl record, printed book, digital / streaming
Melodic death rock. RIYL: Akimbo, Torche, Lungfish, Black Flag

"Brooklyn-by-way-of-Ohio doomsters offer up a big, nasty salute to gas tanks and goat hooves. It all coalesces to form one ravaging feast of melodic death rock that will satiate all your salacious needs, be it Nether-deity worshiping or rock star living." – Broken Beard

☐ **GODMAKER by Godmaker** (ALR 007)
4 song debut LP. Available formats: Vinyl record, printed book, digital / streaming
Doomy sludge metal. RIYL: High on Fire, Red Fang, Mastodon, The Sword

"An example of genuine out of-nowhere brilliance. A patient drawn out campaign of aggression." – Relix

☐ **THE SPACE MERCHANTS by The Space Merchants** (ALR 008)
8 song debut LP. Available formats: Printed book, digital / streaming
Whiskey-soaked space-rock. RIYL: Black Mountain, Dead Meadow, The Besnard Lakes

"A unique brand of lo-fi psych rock... their huge-yet-minimal sound, mixing psych with blues and country style riffs to make something great." – Magnet

☐ **HIRAM-MAXIM by Hiram-Maxim** (ALR 009)
4 song debut LP. Available formats: Vinyl record, printed book, digital / streaming
Noisy experimental doomgaze. RIYL: Swans, Suicide, Pink Floyd, Oxbow

"Builds into an apocalyptic fervor before dissipating into a cloudy haze & ending before you've had your fill." – VICE

☐ **ALTERED STATES OF DEATH AND GRACE by Black Black Black** (ALR 010)
10 song sophomore LP. Available formats: Vinyl record, printed book, digital / streaming
Melodic death rock. RIYL: Akimbo, Torche, Lungfish, Black Flag

"...the kind of good-natured misanthropy of bands like Whores or KEN mode, but the musical gestures beneath the noisy exterior are all forward-charging, Kyuss-worshipping sludge n' roll. It's basically underground metal's version of a radio banger." – BrooklynVegan

☐ **TRESPASSES by Nathaniel Shannon & The Vanishing Twin** (ALR 011)
15 song debut LP. Available formats: Printed book, digital / streaming
Unsettling bedroom recording darkness. RIYL: Lanegan, Badalemnti, Springsteen, Waits

"An unsettling yet captivating collection of songs compiled from a decade of bedroom recordings... Shannon's spoken word-style vocals over haunting and minimalist instrumentals lend a creepy atmosphere to the record." – Decibel

☐ **FERA by Husbandry** (ALR 012)

8 song debut LP. Available formats: Printed book, CD, digital / streaming
Female-fronted math rock meets post-hardcore. RIYL: Mars Volta, Glassjaw, Refused, Deftones

"It's hard to believe that Husbandry is not the biggest band in the world. They're heavy and mathy, chaos wrapped in hard rock and heavy metal." – Nerdist

☐ **MURDEREDMAN by MURDEREDMAN** (ALR 013)

8 song sophomore LP. Available formats: Vinyl record, printed book, digital / streaming
Post-punk inspired noise rock. RIYL: Savages, Bauhaus, Boris, Killing Joke

"A patient and disciplined examination of anxiety and melancholy underpinned with a cathartic tension-and-release structure that borrows from goth, post-metal, and no-wave..." – New Noise Magazine

☐ **IN TENSIONS by Lo-Pan** (ALR 014)

5 song EP. Available formats: Vinyl record, printed book, CD, digital / streaming
Anthemic desert rock. RIYL: Soundgarden, ASG, Torche, Red Fang

"Calling Lo-Pan a stoner band is a disservice to the amalgam of influences the band successfully merges together: the soulful alt rock of the 90s with a thundering doom/sludge sound that's equal parts immediate and timeless." – Nine Circles

☐ **GHOSTS by Hiram-Maxim** (ALR 015)

7 song LP. Available formats: Vinyl record, printed book, digital / streaming
Noisy experimental doomgaze. RIYL: Swans, Suicide, Pink Floyd, Oxbow

"Everything is awash in mesmerizing ambient skree and squalls of atonal feedback. Think an extended, updated version of side 2 of Black Flag's My War." – Hellride Music

☐ **KISS THE DIRT by The Space Merchants** (ALR 016)

10 song sophomore LP. Available formats: Vinyl record, printed book, digital / streaming
Whiskey-soaked space-rock. RIYL: Black Mountain, Dead Meadow, The Besnard Lakes

"[T]he sonic equivalent of having an acid trip in the bathroom between Woodstock and a ZZ Top concert in '69" – New Noise Magazine

☐ **BAD WEEDS NEVER DIE by Husbandry** (ALR 017)

5 song EP. Available formats: Printed book, CD, digital / streaming
Female-fronted math rock meets post-hardcore. RIYL: Mars Volta, Glassjaw, Refused, Deftones

"While retaining their bold go-anywhere style, the EP is a more streamlined and focused effort, signaling a greater maturity and command of recording." – Echoes and Dust

☐ **BY THE GRACE OF BLOOD AND GUTS by Haan** (ALR 018)

8 song LP. Available formats: Printed book, Vinyl, CD, digital / streaming
Noise, Grime, Sludge, Metal, Rock. RIYL: Unsane, Melvins, Swans, Helmet, Clutch

"If Melvins and Unsane had a kid while under the influence of hallucinogens" – Metal Insider

☐ **LUMINOUS VOLUMES by Skryptor** (ALR 019)

7 song LP. Available formats: Vinyl, Printed book, CD, digital / streaming
Noise, Math rock, Prog. RIYL: craw, Dazzling Killmen, Don Cabellero

"Galloping, off-kilter and unabashedly victorious, proggy noise-rock outfit Skryptor's takes hard-rock/psychedelic throwback tropes, flips them on their heads and stretches it all into an adventurous march through endlessly shifting soundscapes."" – Revolver

☐ **DEAD INSIDE by Frayle** (ALR 021)

7 song 7". Alchemy Box: Printed book, Vinyl, CD, digital / streaming
Heavy witch doom. RIYL: Chelsea Wolfe, Portis Head, Sleep, Sunn O)))

"Trades in dark psychedelics and heavy, dripping drums that punctuate the riffing that plays in and around vocalist Gywn Strang's superb voice." – Nine Circles

☐ **SUBTLE by Lo-Pan** (ALR 022)

11 song LP. Available formats: Vinyl, Printed book, CD, digital / streaming
Anthemic desert rock. RIYL: Soundgarden, ASG, Torche, Red Fang

Subtle was produced by James Brown (NIN, Foo Fighters, Ghost) and mastered by Ted Jensen (Mastodon, Deftones, Bad Company, GNR).

☐ 1692 by Frayle (ALR 023)

8 song LP. Available formats: Vinyl, Printed book, CD, digital / streaming
Heavy witch doom. RIYL: Chelsea Wolfe, Portishead, Sleep

"Haunting, hypnotic mix of crushing Sleep-style doom and cooing ethereal vocals à la Cocteau Twins'
Elizabeth Fraser." – Revolver

☐ DESTROYER DELIVER by Zeb Gould (ALR 024)

8 song LP. Available formats: Printed book, CD, digital / streaming
Indie-style gloom-folk meets fingerpicking prairie-bliss. RIYL: Neil Young, Gillian Welch, Bill Callahan

A post-Millenium take on melancholic wasteland love.

☐ THE THREE MOTHERS by Nathaniel Shannon & the Vanishing Twin (ALR 025)

3 song EP. Available formats: Limited Edition Cassette Box, digital / streaming
THE THREE MOTHERS is a primordial fixation with Dario Argento's trilogy's witches. RIYL: Lanegan,
Badalemnti, Springsteen, Tom Waits

"There are very few times that you listen to music and it's something brand new. Something that has
it's own identity and style. Nathaniel Shannon's new EP delivers a passionate dark dreamscape of life.
His leathery dark vocals are ominous as the music that he creates. Close your eyes and you're suddenly
walking down a street with faceless people and distant sound of sirens." – Steve Austin (Today is the Day
/ Austin Enterprises)

☐ PRISONER'S CINEMA by Burning Tongue (ALR 026)

11 song LP. Available formats: Vinyl, Printed book, CD, digital / streaming
Crushing nihilism that nod to the shadowy side of hardcore punk. RIYL: Power Trip, Craft, G.I.S.M.

With chainsaw guitars, pummeling double-bass and a barking prophet preaching an end times message,
Burning Tongue is here to remind you that the plague has arrived and rain piss all over your pitiful
socially-distanced BBQs, park hangs and elbow daps.

JOIN THE AQUALAMB RESEARCH CLUB

A record company like Aqualamb releases many albums and books each year. Some of them are by
long established artists while others are by people no one has heard of but us. In either case, we'd
like to try out some of our upcoming music on you. After all you are the consumer. The final decision
is always yours.

So we'd like to know what you think just a little bit earlier. You might say, we'd like to put you into
our A&R Department with a little service we call Aqualamb Research Club. Aqualamb Research
Club is a series of songs we'll be sending out over the course of a year. On each one you'll get a
sampling of brand-new or unreleased albums. Each issue of Aqualamb Research Club comes a
minimal-baloney newsletter telling you what we and our artists have been up to lately.

Your role in Aqualamb Research Club is simple. All we want is to hear from you—what you like, what
you hate, and why. A year of Aqualamb Research Club will cost you 10 bucks, which just about
covers packaging and mailing. In return, you will get a lot of fine music, an Aqualamb T-shirt, and
a special Aqualamb Research Club pin plus the chance to influence the course of music.

No strings, no gimmicks, no dumb offers or obligations. We just want to tune in to your taste.

EMAIL INFO@AQUALAMB.ORG FOR MORE INFO ON HOW YOU CAN BE A PART OF OUR RESEARCH.

Aqualamb

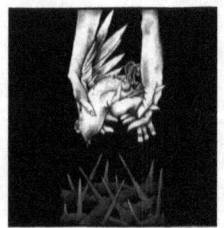

The music for *Destroyer Deliver*
can be downloaded via the link below:

aqualamb.org/024